AN AMERICAN TAIL ™·
Fievel and Tiger

by **Michael Teitelbaum**

From a screenplay by **Judy Freudberg & Tony Geiss**
Based upon characters created b~~y David~~ **Kirschner**
Based on animated characte
Illustrated by **David**
Beverly Lazor-
Christine Fi~~~~

AMBLIN
ENTERTAINMENT

Fievel Mousekewitz was a little mouse with a great big sense of adventure. He had just arrived in America from Russia, and he was very busy exploring New York City.

Sometimes his exploring and his sense of adventure got him into trouble.

One day, Fievel was standing on his toes trying to look into a window. He stretched and stretched until he could see in.

Inside, Fievel saw a group of mean-looking cats called The Mott Street Maulers. The cats were sitting around a large table playing cards.

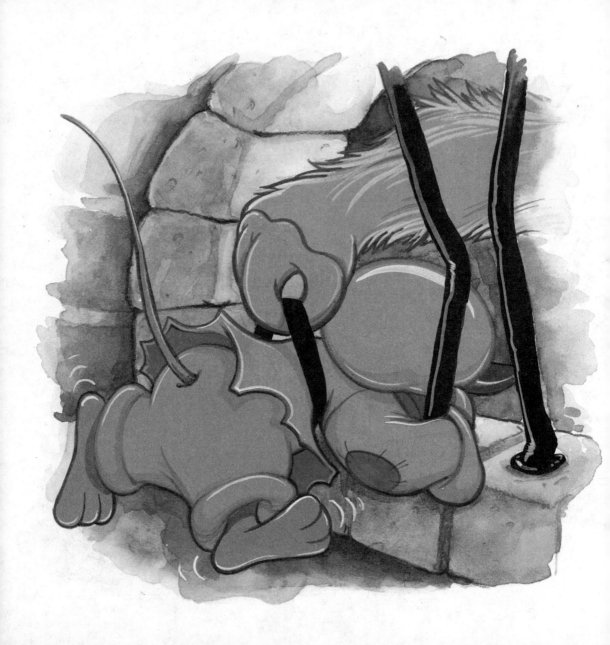

Just then, one of the cats reached through the window and grabbed Fievel.

"I got you," growled the cat. "And now you're trapped!" He took Fievel and locked him in a cage.

The cage was placed in another room, and a big cat named Tiger was put in the room to guard Fievel.

"Don't make any funny moves," snarled Tiger. "I'm quick and I'm clever. Just like a cat. What am I saying? I am a cat!"

Fievel began to cry.

"Hey," said Tiger. "What are you crying about?"

"I'll never get out of here," sobbed the little mouse. "Are you and your friends going to eat me?"

"Eat you!" exclaimed Tiger. "Why, I wouldn't do that."

"You wouldn't?" asked Fievel, who stopped crying and was feeling a little better.

"I think you're nice," said Tiger. "You know, I don't have anything against mice. I like mice. Not for dinner, I mean. I don't eat mice, I'm a vegetarian."

"That's great," said Fievel. "I thought all cats were supposed to be mean and hate mice."

"Mean? Not me!" shouted Tiger. "I'm a nice guy, when you get to know me. I really am."

"I think we probably have a lot in common," said Tiger. "I like butterflies with big golden wings, and blue and green tips."

"Me too!" shouted Fievel.

"I also love Swiss cheese ice cream," added Tiger.

"Yum, my favorite!" said Fievel. "I think we could be friends!"

"Yeah," smiled Tiger. "I never had any friends."

Suddenly Fievel grew sad once more.

"Hey! What's the matter, old chum?" asked Tiger.

"I just remembered those friends of yours, The Mott Street Maulers," said Fievel. "When they come back, I'll be in trouble."

Tiger looked all around the room. "I'll tell you what," he said. "I'll open the cage door and look the other way. You run off."

"Would you really do that?" asked Fievel.

"Sure," asked Tiger. "What are friends for?"

Tiger opened the door to the cage and Fievel hopped out.

"Thank you, Tiger," said Fievel, as they warmly hugged each other. "I'll never forget this."

"You'd better hurry," said Tiger, "before the other cats come."

With that, Fievel scurried to the window and ran out. He was free. On his way home, he thought about how unusual and wonderful it was that a cat and a mouse could become good friends.